THIS BOOK BELONGS to

....

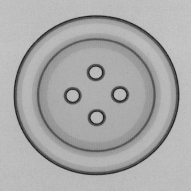

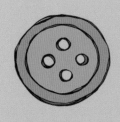

THE Little Stripey Button

written by Jess Ives

Illustrated by M Venn

Our story begins in a little red box,
where a little stripey button feels lonely and lost,

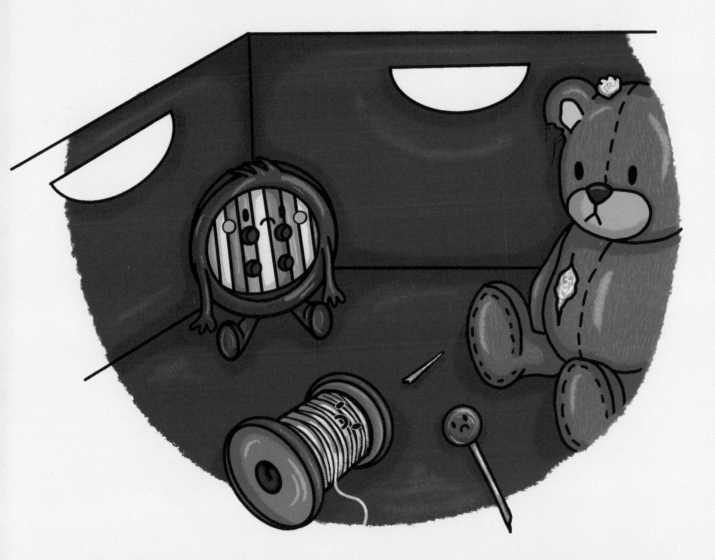

Everyday he sits there, with the cotton and thread,
the little broken pin and scruffy old ted.

"I must find my place,
what can I be?
I need to escape,
I want to be free."

As he struggles about
in the little red box,
it suddenly rips and out
tumbles the lot.

"I'm free at last, where
can I go, to find what
i'm looking for?"
he just doesn't know.

So feeling a little nervous,
he rolls across the floor,
under the table and
out through the door.

2

Down the stairs he carefully goes,
and stops by a cat, twitching her nose.

"Excuse me" he asks, shouting quite loud,
"Can you tell me the place, where the soldiers stand proud?"

The cat just sits there, with nothing to say,
so the little stripey button goes on his way.

The little stripey button has always had a dream,
to be sewed to a jacket, the grandest you've seen.
Now the buttons he's seen are as gold, as can be,
"maybe, just maybe they will still want me."

He rolls along passing people and shops,
then sees a sign and suddenly stops.

There on the sign, is the jacket he needs
"Buckingham Palace this way" are the words that he reads.
With an excitable bounce, he carries on his way,
will they want him, what will they say?

He finally comes to a building so tall,
he looks around feeling scared and small.
There by the gate, standing proud and bold,
is a very fine soldier, with buttons so gold.

The little stripey button shouts out loud
"Can I please join you? I want to stand proud"
The shiny gold buttons look down from the jacket,
and just start to laugh, asking "what is that racket?"

"You are not the right button, not shiny or gold,
too stripey and bright, too colourful and bold."
The little stripey button just rolls away
feeling sad and upset, not knowing what to say.

He rolls along feeling lost and alone,
doesn't know where he is, doesn't know the way home.

The little stripey button is as sad as can be,
as the rain starts to fall, he rests by a tree.
He's very cold and wet so snuggles into the leaves,
falls fast asleep and starts to dream.

The little stripey button doesn't feel the hand,
of the little boy passing in the jacket so grand.

"This is just perfect,
it's stripey and bright,
it's not boring or ordinary,
it's colourful, just right".

The little stripey button then opens his eyes,
he's no longer cold and wet, but warm and dry.

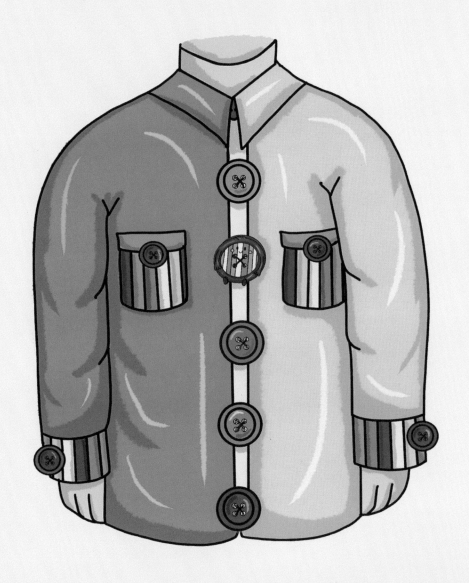

Sitting proudly on a jacket, of red, blue, yellow and green,
the most wonderful jacket he has ever seen.

So, now we will leave the little stripey button,
who is as happy as can be,
just remember there's a place in this world,
for everyone including you and me.

Before Reading

* Talk about the title and picture on the front cover.

* Look through the pictures together and discuss what you think
the story might be about.

After Reading

* Discuss and talk about why the little stripey button feels lonely
and lost.

* Talk about your child's emotions, have they
ever felt sad, lonely or lost.

* Ask your child, who lives at Buckingham Palace?

* Ask your child, how does the little stripey
button become happy again?

* Discuss what might happen next in the story.

more titles to follow

Let's find out what happened
when the scruffy old ted,
cotton and thread and little broken pin
tumbled out of the box...

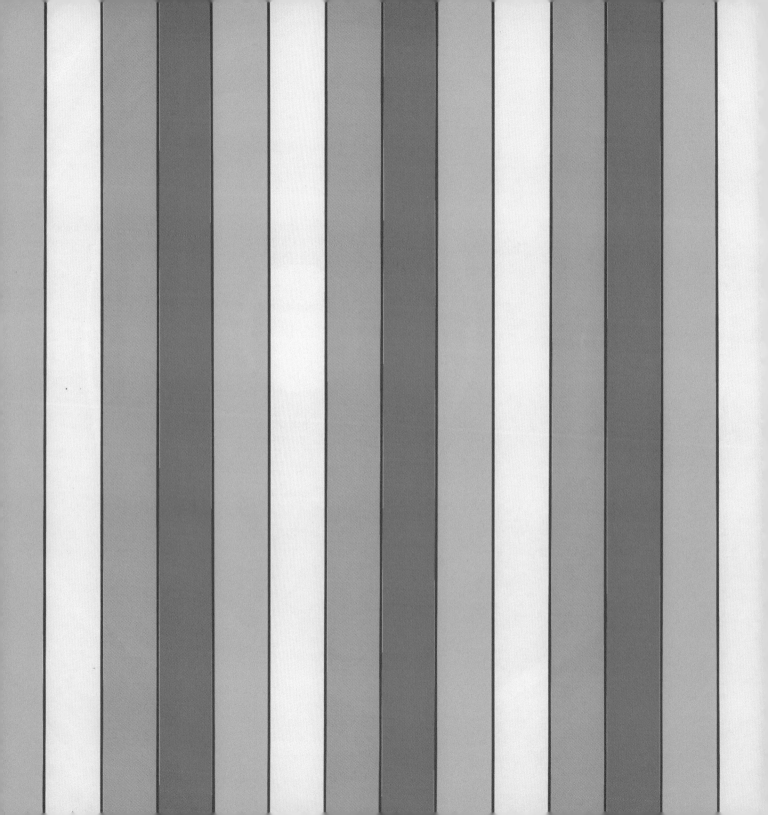

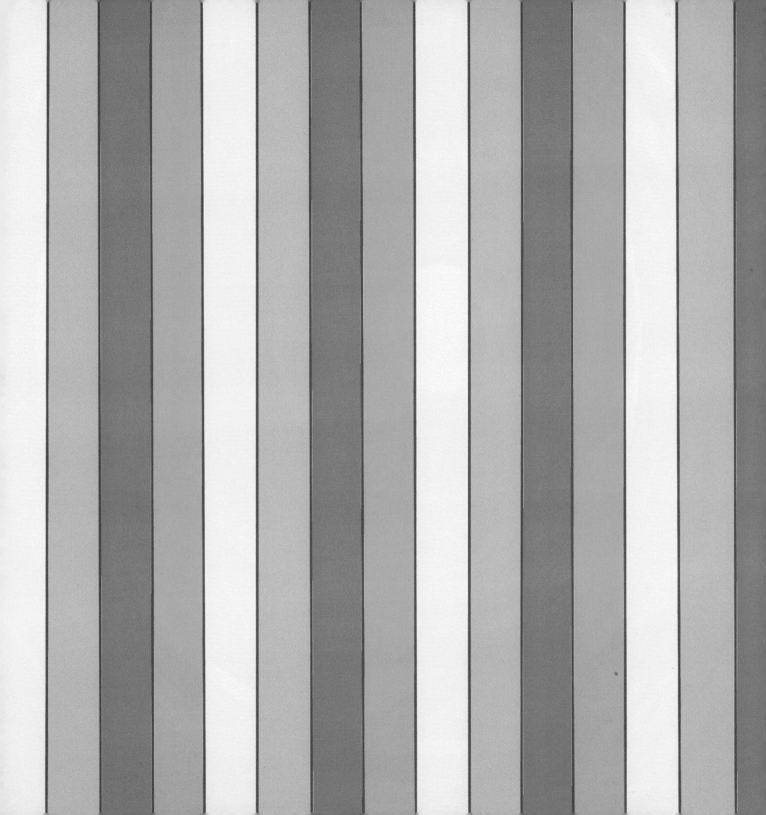

Printed in Great Britain
by Amazon